Eddie

Davy

Nicky

Donny

Daisy

Copyright © 1999 by Nord-Süd Verlag AG, Gossau, Zürich, Switzerland
First published in Switzerland under the title *Pauli Streit mit Edi*
English translation copyright © 1999 by North-South Books Inc.

First published in the United States, Great Britain, Canada,
Australia, and New Zealand in 1999 by North-South Books,
an imprint of Nord-Süd Verlag AG, Gossau Zürich, Switzerland.

Distributed in the United States by North-South Books Inc., New York.

Library of Congress Cataloging-in-Publication Data is available.
A CIP catalogue record for this book is available from The British Library.

ISBN 0-7358-1073-7 (trade binding) 10 9 8 7 6 5 4 3 2 1
ISBN 0-7358-1074-5 (library binding) 10 9 8 7 6 5 4 3 2 1

Printed in Belgium

For more information about our books, and the authors and artists
who create them, visit our web site: http://www.northsouth.com

Why Are You Fighting, Davy?

By Brigitte Weninger
Illustrated by Eve Tharlet

Translated by Rosemary Lanning

A MICHAEL NEUGEBAUER BOOK
NORTH-SOUTH BOOKS / NEW YORK / LONDON

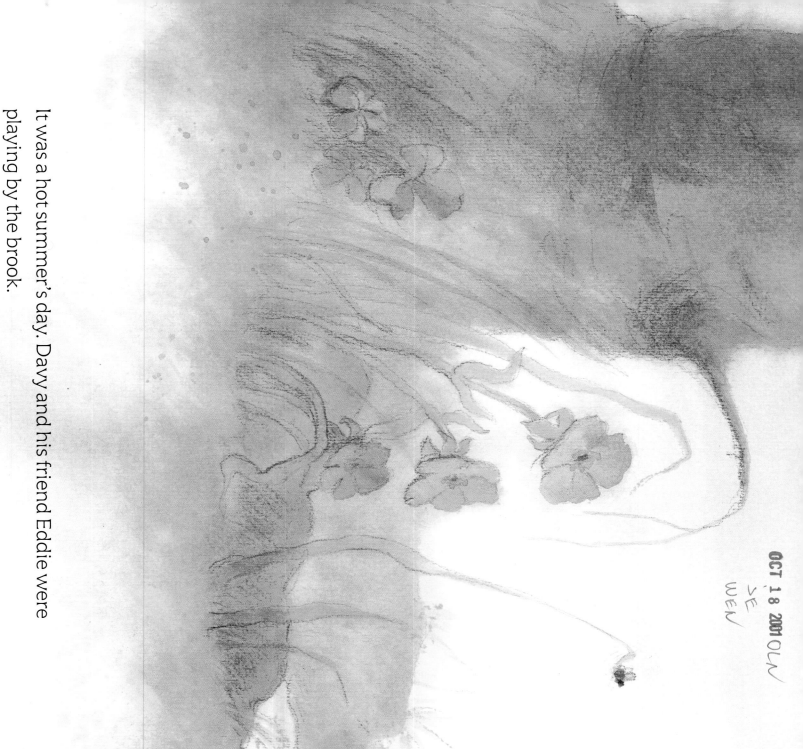

It was a hot summer's day. Davy and his friend Eddie were playing by the brook.

"Let's build a dam," Eddie suggested.

"I don't know how," said Davy.

"Leave it to me!" said Eddie. "I build the best dams in the world."

"All right," said Davy. "You build the dam and I'll make a boat. I build the best boats in the world."

They both set to work.

Eddie was nearly finished with the dam, and Davy had made a big boat out of twigs and bark. He proudly showed it to Eddie.

"Launch it, if you like," said Eddie.

"I just need a couple more rocks. Then the dam will be ready."

The water level was rising behind the dam.

"Will it be strong enough?" asked Davy doubtfully. "Of course," said Eddie. "My dams are always strong enough."

At that moment, the dam burst.

The sudden rush of water swept Davy's boat away.

"My boat! My beautiful boat!" wailed Davy. He ran after it, but the water was moving too fast for him to catch up. Davy came back, furious. "That was the best boat I ever built!" he shouted. "Now it's gone, and it's all your fault!"

"It was just a silly little boat!" Eddie retorted. "I could make one with my eyes closed!"

This was too much for Davy. He pulled Eddie's ear, and Eddie pulled his, and then they were both on the ground, rolling over and over until they tumbled into the cold brook. That stopped them!

Davy stood up and shook the water off.

"That's it, Eddie!" he said. "You're not my friend anymore. I never want to see you again. Never ever!"

And he ran all the way home.

"Back already?" said Davy's mother, surprised to see him home so soon.

"I thought you were playing with Eddie."

"We had a fight. I'm never going to play with him, ever again," said Davy.

"Oh dear," said Mother Rabbit.

"Why were you fighting, Davy?"

"He wrecked my boat," said Davy.

"But Davy," said his mother, shaking her head, "Eddie is your best friend."

"He was my best friend," said Davy, and he stormed off.

Davy went to his room to find his toy rabbit, Nicky.

"You're my best friend, Nicky," he said. "We never fight, do we? Do you want to play?"

Nicky didn't say no. So Davy threw him up in the air and caught him. Then he threw him again and again, until his arms began to ache. After that they played hide-and-seek, but Davy had to do all the seeking. Nicky wasn't much good at tag, either.

Davy said, "Nicky, I do like you, but this is boring. Let's see if Dan or Donny or Daisy wants to play."

Davy found his big brother Dan at the front door.

"Will you play with us, Dan?" he said.

"Not now. I'm going to meet my friends," said Dan.

So Davy went to look for Daisy and Donny, but he couldn't find them. He asked his mother where they were.

"They've gone to pick mushrooms with your father," said Mother Rabbit. "Why not play with Dinah while I do the washing?"

Davy didn't want to play with Dinah. She was just a baby. He scowled and walked away. "Let's go back to the brook, Nicky," he said.

Davy set Nicky down at the water's edge.

"Watch this," he said. "I'll show you how to build a dam. If Eddie can do it, so can I."

Davy waded into the brook.

He piled stones on top of each other, but they all fell down, and the water wouldn't stop flowing through his dam.

Davy tried and tried again. He was getting hot and bothered.

"How did Eddie do it?" he muttered.

Just then a wobbly little boat floated past, half sunk in the water.

"Where did that come from?" Davy wondered. "Come on, Nicky. Let's find out!"

Davy tiptoed upstream and saw Eddie, trying to launch another boat. The boat kept falling over.

Eddie tried and tried again. He was getting hot and bothered.

"How did Davy do it?" he muttered.

"Simple," said Davy. "You have to put the main mast right in the middle."

Eddie looked up, startled. "I can't do this as well as you," he said.

"Do you want me to help you?" asked Davy.

"Yes, please!"

Davy showed Eddie what he was doing wrong, and together they built two big, beautiful bark boats.

"We need a pool to float these on,"
said Davy. "I started to build a dam,
but I can't do it as well as you."

"Do you want me to
help you?" asked Eddie.

"Yes, please!"

Eddie showed Davy how to wedge
the stones securely, and together
they built a big, strong dam right
across the brook.

As the water level rose behind the dam, the two friends whooped for joy.

"It's holding! It's holding!" cried Davy.

Then they solemnly shook hands.

"You did a good job, Davy."

"So did you, Eddie."

They played with their boats until the sun went down.

When Davy came home, the rest of his family was already at the supper table.

"Why did you stay out so late, Davy?" asked Mother Rabbit.

"I was playing in the brook with Eddie," he said. "It was such fun, we forgot the time."

"You played with Eddie?" said Mother. "I thought you two had a fight."

"Oh, that was ages ago," said Davy.

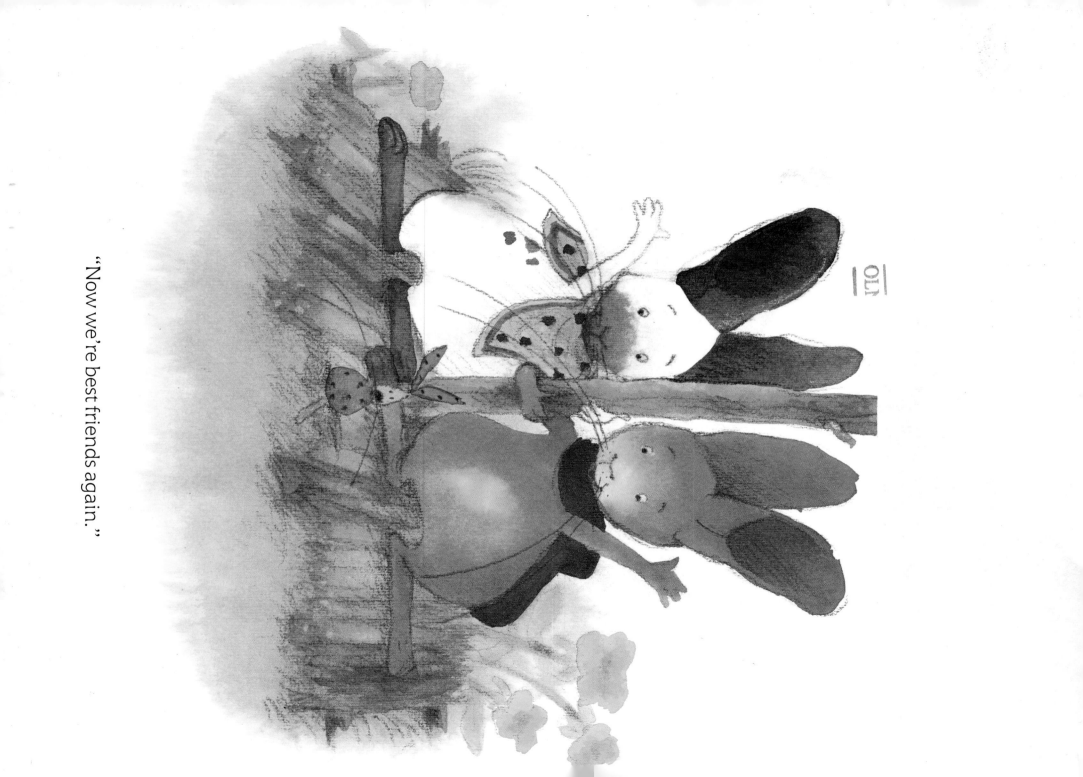

"Now we're best friends again."